Grandma's BIRD

By Jack Gabolinscy

Illustrated by Astrid Matijasevich

Grandma's BIRD

Everybody was sad when Grandpa died. Grandma cried, Mom and Dad cried, and I cried, too. I held Grandma's hand so she didn't feel so bad.

Next day Mom and I visited Grandma. When she saw us, she started crying again. I knew she was lonely because Grandpa was gone.

I said, "You can have one of my birds, Grandma. Then you won't be lonely."

"Shhh!" said Mom. "Leave Grandma alone."

Grandma smiled through her tears. "What a good idea," she said. "I'd like that."

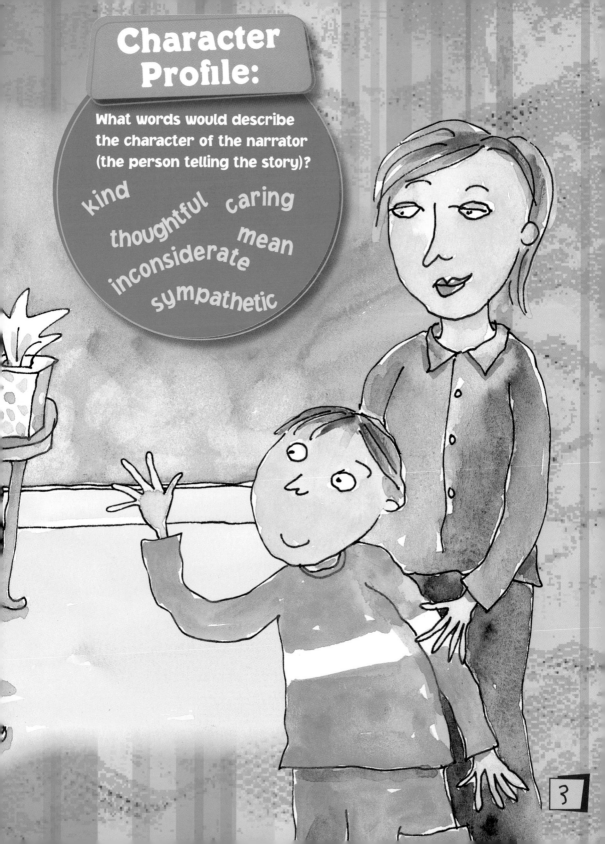

I gave Grandma a pretty blue and white bird. He was the funniest and noisiest of them all. She put his cage on the table next to her rocking chair.

"I'll call him Peter, after Grandpa," she said.

Grandma and Peter became good friends. Grandma laughed when he hung upside down on his swing and rang his bell. She laughed when he looked in his mirror and squawked loudly as if he were talking to a friend.

Grandma loved watching Peter fly round in circles when she let him out to stretch his wings. She laughed when he flew down and landed on her head. She even laughed when it was time for him to go back into his cage and he wouldn't go.

Question:

Why do you think the narrator gave Grandma the funniest, noisiest bird?

5

Grandma said, "I'll teach Peter to talk."

"Birds can't talk," I told her.

But I was wrong. Before long, Peter was talking, like a nonstop wind-up CD deck on fast speed.

"Peter's a pretty boy! Peter's a pretty boy! Peter's a pretty boy!"

Soon he could say lots of words. Whenever there was a quiet moment, his funny voice sang out through Grandma's living room.

Good morning, Grandma!

Hello! Hello! Hello!

Bedtime, Peter!

Yummy cracker!

Wake up, Grandma!

Sometimes when there were strangers around, Peter got excited. He bobbed up and down and strutted around his cage, like a famous film star on a stage.

"Hello! Hello! Quark! Quark! Who's a pretty boy? Bedtime, Peter! Pop goes the weasel. Quark! Quark! Good morning, Grandma! Mary had a little lamb! Hello! Hello! Hello! Pop goes the weasel! Quark! Quark! Quark!"

Peter made Grandma happy. She treated him like a spoiled baby, always buying new toys for his cage or giving him new birdseed.

She talked to him continuously. "Who's a pretty boy? Who's a pretty boy?" she asked.

"Yummy cracker! Yummy cracker! Pop goes the weasel! Yummy cracker," he replied, bobbing up and down like a funny little boy.

Simile:

A simile compares one thing to another by using the words "like" or "as", and often creates a mental picture in the reader's mind.

Can you find a simile ?

9

Then one day, Grandma got sick and had to go to the hospital. She lay on the pillow – a plastic mask on her nose and her eyes closed. There were tubes in her arms and a big bag hanging behind her. When she breathed, it sounded like a fireman breathing through a rescue mask.

Every day on my way home from school, I visited Peter and fed him and let him out to stretch his wings. I told him that Grandma would be home soon. "She misses you!" I said. "She can't wait to see you again."

"Hello! Hello! Yummy cracker! Pop goes the weasel! Wake up, Grandma. Quark! Quark!" replied Peter.

Predict:

What do you think will happen in the story now?

Every night, Mom took me to see Grandma. She would sleep, and her breath would come out as a deep, husky, empty sound through her mask. "Peter says he loves you," I told Grandma. "He wants you to come home soon." She didn't answer . . . but I knew she could hear.

Mom and I visited Grandma every night for a long time. Every night I held Grandma's hand and listened to her loud breathing inside her mask. "Shhuuuushh! Shhhuuushh!" Every night I told Grandma, "Peter loves you, Grandma. He wants you to come home."

"She's not getting better," the doctor told Mom. "We can't do anything more."

Mom cried when she told Dad. "The doctors are doing all they can," she said. "There's nothing more we can do."

Clarify:

husky

A wheezy
B throaty/hoarse
C loud

A, B, or C ?

13

That night in bed, I cried when I thought about Grandma. I knew there was something more I could do. I knew how to make her better. "Tomorrow, Grandma," I promised. "Tomorrow I will make you well."

Next morning I went to Grandma's house to feed Peter and let him out for a fly. "Hello, Peter," I said.

"Yummy cracker! Yummy cracker! Pop goes the weasel!" He was excited to see me. "Pop goes the weasel! Pop goes the weasel! Pop goes the weasel! Quark! Quark! Quark! Wake up, Grandma!"

I carried Peter to the hospital in his cage.

Question:

Why do you think the narrator/boy took the budgie to the hospital?

I went up in the elevator and walked along the corridor toward Grandma's room. "You talk to her, Peter. You tell her to get better."

"Pop goes the weasel!" sang Peter in his funny voice.

Then, just as I got to Grandma's door, a doctor stopped me. "Hey! Young man!" she said. "You can't take a bird in there. That lady is sick. You will make her worse."

She took me by the arm and started to lead me away from Grandma's room. "No! No!" I cried. "Peter won't make Grandma sick. He's her best friend. He'll make her better."

"I'm sorry," said the doctor. "I can't let you take a bird in there. It's against the rules."

Inference:

What can you infer about the character of the doctor from the following words?
"I can't let you take a bird in there. It's against the rules."

16

I wanted to cry. I tried to break away from the doctor and run back to Grandma's room, but she wouldn't let me, so I sat down on the floor and cried anyway.

Peter thought I wanted to play and got excited. "Quark! Quark! Quark!" he squawked in his funny voice, bobbing up and down across his swing. "Wake up, Grandma! Wake up, Grandma! Yummy cracker! Quark! Quark! Wake up, Grandma! Wake up, Grandma! Wake up, Grandma!"

The doctor heard Peter showing off and started laughing. "I see what you mean," she said. "He must be a very good friend."

The doctor looked at me and Peter for a long time . . .

Action and Response:

The doctor said the narrator could not take Peter into Grandma's room.	→	The narrator sat down on the floor and cried.
Peter got excited and started to show off.	→	?

"Look," she said at last. "Maybe you are right. Maybe Peter's medicine can do what my medicine can't do."

I walked back along the corridor with the doctor to Grandma's room. I put Peter's cage on a table near the window, in the sun beside her bed.

For once Peter was quiet. He stood on his swing looking around the room. He had a drink of water. He pecked at his mirror. He jumped onto a perch and scratched the feathers under his eye.

"Come on, Peter," I said. "Say something!"

"Perhaps he's shy in front of strangers," said the doctor.

"No," I said. "He likes to show off. He's a big ham!"

"Come on, Peter! Say something," I begged.

Emotions:

How did the narrator feel when Peter went quiet?

upset
anxious   concerned
thoughtful   worried
hopeful
confident

He's a big ham!

Peter started walking backward
and forward along his perch.
Faster and faster he strutted,
his head bobbing up and down, up
and down, up and down.

"Wake up, Grandma!" he
screeched. "Wake up, Grandma!
Wake up, Grandma! Quark!
Quark! Yummy cracker! Pop goes
the weasel! Wake up, Grandma!
Wake up, Grandma! Quark!
Quark! Quark!"

The doctor laughed. "I see what
you mean," she said. "He really
is a show-off."

"Wake up, Grandma! Wake up,
Grandma! Wake up, Grandma!"
Peter screeched.

But Grandma didn't move.
She lay still on her pillow.
"Shuuuuush! Shuuuuush!
Shuuuuush!" sounded her breath
inside her mask.

"Wake up, Grandma! Wake up,
Grandma!"

Synonym:

A synonym is a word that means the same as another word.

Which word is the synonym for strutted?

A wandered

B walked with a deliberate stride

C ran

A, B, or C ?

I watched Grandma, hoping for a miracle. But she didn't move. She didn't say anything. She just kept breathing loudly. "Keep talking, Peter! Don't stop!" I said.

"Shuuuuuush! Shuuuush!" breathed Grandma.

The doctor patted me on the head. "Don't expect too much," she said. "Your Grandma is very sick. Even Peter may not be able to make her well."

Wake up, Grandma!

Wake up, Grandma!

Wake up, Grandma!

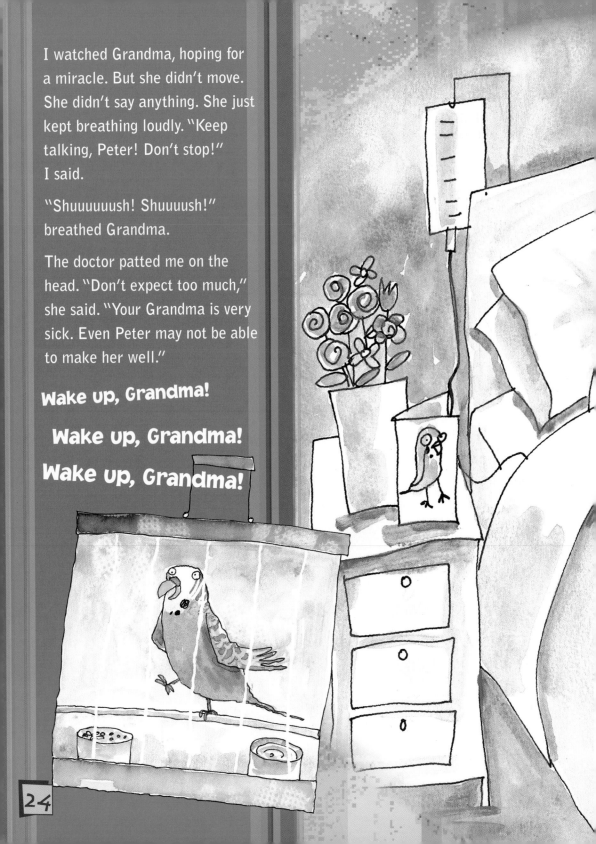

She just kept breathing loudly.

25

Emotions:

What words would you use to describe how the narrator is feeling now?

calm

frustrated

desperate

angry

unhappy

sad

anxious

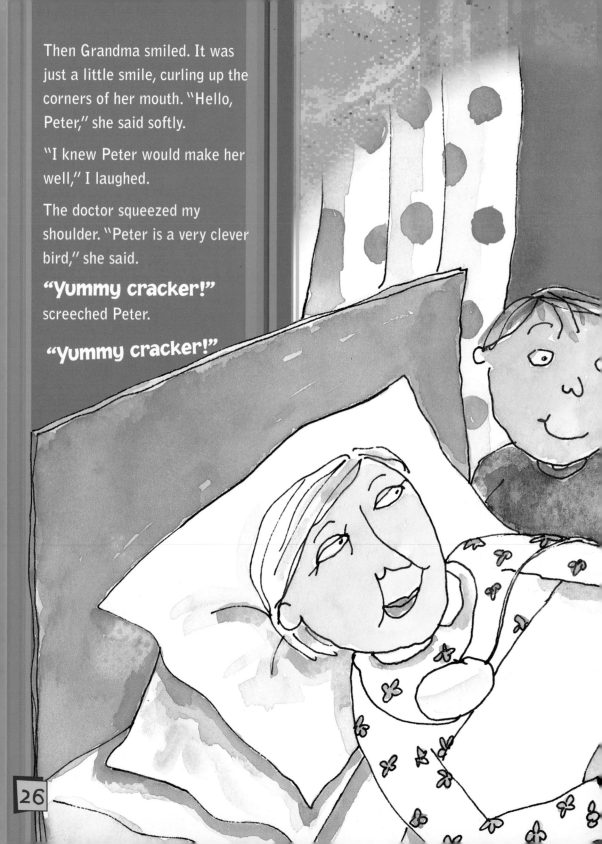

Then Grandma smiled. It was just a little smile, curling up the corners of her mouth. "Hello, Peter," she said softly.

"I knew Peter would make her well," I laughed.

The doctor squeezed my shoulder. "Peter is a very clever bird," she said.

"Yummy cracker!" screeched Peter.

"Yummy cracker!"

26

Summary:

What key points would you put in a summary of *Grandma's Bird*?

- The narrator gave Grandma a bird so she wouldn't be lonely.

- Grandma taught the bird to talk.

- Grandma got sick and went to the hospital.

- The doctor said Grandma wasn't getting better.

- The narrator took the bird to visit Grandma in the hospital.

- The doctor said birds were not allowed in the hospital.

- The narrator cried.

- The bird made the doctor laugh and was allowed into the hospital.

- Grandma woke up and smiled at the bird.

Think About the Text

Making connections – What connections can you make to the text?

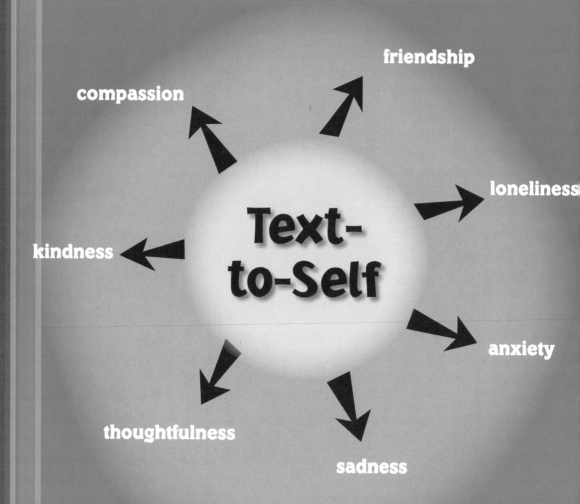

friendship

compassion

loneliness

kindness

Text-to-Self

anxiety

thoughtfulness

sadness

Text-to-Text

Talk about other stories you may have read that have similar features. Compare the stories.

Text-to-World

Talk about situations in the world that might connect to elements in the story.

Planning a Personal Recount

① Think about an introduction

Think about:

Who

When

. . . when I was a kid

Where

. . . at the hospital

What

② Think about events in order of sequence

The narrator gave Grandma a bird so she wouldn't be lonely.	→ Grandma got sick and went to the hospital.	→ The doctor said Grandma wasn't getting better.
The narrator took the bird to visit Grandma in the hospital.	→ The doctor said birds were not allowed in the hospital.	→ The bird made the doctor laugh and was allowed into the hospital.

③ Think about the conclusion

Grandma woke up and smiled at the bird.

In a Personal Recount ...

A the narrator's own responses and reactions are recorded

B events are recorded in a sequence, and links to time are made

C events all relate to one particular occasion, happening, or idea

D there is a conclusion at the end, that could include an interpretation of events or a personal comment

E past tense is used

F first person is used

G the narrator was personally involved in the event